Clever Chick

Paul Shipton
Illustrated by Trevor Dunton

Pip was a clever chick.
One day, she went for a walk.

Pip saw a fox.

She ran away as fast as she could,

but the fox ran faster.

"Hello, little chick," said the fox.
"You can't run away from me.
I am faster than you."

"You may be faster than I am," said Pip,
"but I am stronger than you!"

Pip picked up a small stick.
She lifted it over her head.

The fox laughed.

"Don't be silly," he said.

"I am much stronger than you."

He picked up a bigger stick.

"OK," said Pip. "You are stronger than I
am, but I can jump higher than you can."
She jumped up in the air.

The fox laughed again.

"Don't be silly," he said.

"I can jump much higher than you can."

The fox jumped up into the sky.

"OK," said Pip.
"You can jump higher than I can,
but I can shout louder than you can."
She cheeped as loudly as she could.

The fox was very angry. "This is **very** silly!
I can shout **much** louder than you can!"

The fox howled.

He howled and howled.

He was **very** loud.

A farmer heard the howl.

He ran after the fox.

The fox ran away as fast as he could.

Pip walked on. She said to herself,
"The fox is faster and stronger than I am.
He can jump higher than I can,
and he can shout louder than I can . . .

but I'm **clever**!"